When everyone was asleep Witch Baby crept back into the cottage, went into the violet-and-aqua-tiled bathroom and stared at herself in the mirror. She saw a messy nest of hair, a pale, skinny body, knobby, skinned knees and feet with curling toes.

No wonder Raphael doesn't love me, Witch Baby thought. I am a baby witch.

She took the toenail scissors and began to chop at her own hair. Then she plugged in My Secret Agent Lover Man's razor, turned it on and listened to it buzz at her like a hungry metal animal.

When her scalp was completely bald, Witch Baby, with her deep-set, luminous, jacaranda-blossom-colored eyes, looked as if she had drifted down from some other planet.

But Witch Baby did not see her eerie, fairy, genie, moon-witch beauty, the beauty of twilight and rainstorms. "You'll never belong to anyone," she said to the bald girl in the mirror. . . .

---

witch baby

witch baby

FRANCESCA LIA BLOCK

A Charlotte Zolotow Book

Francesca Lia Block

HarperKeypoint
An Imprint of HarperCollinsPublishers

Library of Congress Cataloging-in-Publication Data
Block, Francesca Lia.
  Witch Baby / Francesca Lia Block.
    p.   cm.
  "A Charlotte Zolotow book."
  Summary: Witch Baby comes to live with Weetzie Bat and My-Se-
cret-Agent-Lover-Man and has wild adventures in Los Angeles as she
tries to understand where she belongs.
  ISBN 0-06-020547-4. — ISBN 0-06-020548-2 (lib. bdg.)
  ISBN 0-06-447065-2 (pbk.)
  [1. Identity—Fiction.   2. Los Angeles (Calif.)—Fiction.]
I. Title.
PZ7.B61945Wi   1991   90-28916
[Fic]—dc20   CIP
                                                             AC

Harper Keypoint is an imprint of Harper Trophy, a division of
HarperCollins Publishers. First Harper Keypoint edition, 1992.

For My Mother

and with thanks to Randi Shutan,

in Memory

Contents

witch baby

Once, in a city called Shangri-L.A. or Hell-A or just Los Angeles, lived Weetzie Bat, the daughter of Brandy-Lynn and Charlie Bat. A genie granted Weetzie three wishes, so she wished for a Duck for her best friend Dirk McDonald, "My Secret Agent Lover Man for me," and a little house for them all to live in happily ever after. The wishes came true, mostly. Dirk met Duck Drake and Weetzie met My Secret Agent Lover Man and they all lived together. When Weetzie wanted a baby and My Secret Agent Lover Man didn't, Dirk and Duck helped her, and Cherokee was born. My Secret was angry and went away. He stayed with Vixanne Wigg for a while, but he loved Weetzie so much that he returned. One day Vixanne left a basket on the porch of the house where Weetzie and My Secret Agent Lover Man and the baby, Cherokee, and Dirk and Duck all lived. In the basket was Witch Baby and this is her story.

Upon Time

Once upon a time. What is that supposed to mean?

In the room full of musical instruments, watercolor paints, candles, sparkles, beads, books, basketballs, roses, incense, surfboards, china pixie heads, lanky toy lizards and a rubber chicken, Witch Baby was curling her toes, tapping her drumsticks and pulling on the snarl balls in her hair. Above her hung the clock, luminous, like a moon.

Witch Baby had taken photographs of everyone in her almost-family—Weetzie Bat and My Secret Agent Lover Man, Cherokee Bat, Dirk McDonald and Duck Drake, Valentine, Ping Chong and Raphael Chong Jah-Love, Brandy-Lynn Bat and Coyote Dream Song. Then she had scrambled up the fireplace and pasted the pictures on the numbers of the clock. Because she had taken all the pictures herself, there was no witch child with dark tangled hair and tilted purple eyes.

What time are we upon and where do I belong? Witch Baby wondered as she went into the garden.

The peach trees, rosebushes and purple-flowering jacaranda were sparkling with strings of white lights. Witch Baby watched from behind the garden shed as her almost-family danced on the lawn, celebrating the completion of *Dangerous Angels*, a movie they had made about their lives. In *Angels*, Weetzie Bat met her best friend Dirk and wished on a genie lamp for "a Duck for Dirk and My Secret Agent Lover Man for me and a beautiful little house for us to live in happily ever after." The movie was about what happened when the wishes came true.

Witch Baby's almost-mother-and-father, Weetzie Bat and My Secret Agent Lover Man, were doing a cha-cha on the lawn. In a short pink evening gown, pink Harlequin sunglasses and a white feathered headdress, Weetzie looked like a strawberry sundae melting into My Secret Agent Lover Man's arms. Dirk Mc-Donald was dancing with Duck Drake and pretending to balance his champagne glass on Duck's perfect blonde flat-top. Weetzie's mother, Brandy-Lynn Bat, was dancing with My Secret Agent Lover Man's best friend, Coyote. Valentine Jah-Love and his wife, Ping Chong, swayed together, while their Hershey's-powdered-chocolate-mix-colored son, Raphael Chong Jah-Love, danced with Weetzie's real daughter, Cherokee Bat. Even Slinkster Dog and Go-Go Girl were dancing, raised up circus style on their hind legs, wriggling their rears and surrounded by their puppies, Pee Wee, Wee Wee, Teenie Wee, Tiki Tee and Tee Pee, who were not really puppies anymore but had never gotten any bigger than when they were six months old.

Under the twinkling trees was a table covered with Guatemalan fabric, roses in juice jars, wax rose candles from Tijuana and plates of food—Weetzie's Vegetable Love-Rice, My Secret Agent Lover Man's guacamole, Dirk's homemade pizza, Duck's fig and berry salad and Surfer Surprise Protein Punch, Brandy-Lynn's pink macaroni, Coyote's cornmeal cakes, Ping's mushu plum crepes and Valentine's Jamaican plantain pie.

Witch Baby's stomach growled but she didn't leave her hiding place. Instead, she listened to the reggae, surf, soul and salsa, tugged at the snarl balls in her hair and snapped pictures of all the couples. She wanted to dance but there was no one to dance with. There was only Rubber Chicken lying around somewhere inside the cottage. He always seemed to end up being her only partner.

After a while, Weetzie and My Secret Agent Lover Man sat down near the shed. Witch

Baby watched them. Sometimes she thought she looked a little like My Secret Agent Lover Man; but she knew he and Weetzie had found her on their doorstep one day. Witch Baby didn't look like Weetzie Bat at all.

"What's wrong, my slinkster-love-man?" Witch Baby heard Weetzie ask as she handed My Secret Agent Lover Man a paper plate sagging with food. "Aren't you happy that we finished *Angels*?"

He lit a cigarette and stared past the party into the darkness. Shadows of roses moved across his angular face.

"The movie wasn't enough," he said. "We have more money now than we know what to do with. Sometimes this city feels like an expensive tomb. I want to do something that matters."

"But you speak with your movies," Weetzie said. "You are an important influence on people. You open eyes."

"It hasn't been enough. I need to think of something strong. When I was a kid I had a lamp shaped like a globe. I had newspaper articles all over my walls, too, like Witch Baby has—disasters and things. I always wished I could make the world as peaceful and bright as my lamp."

"Give yourself time," said Weetzie, and she took off his slouchy fedora, pushed back his dark hair and kissed his temples.

Witch Baby wished that she could go and sit on Weetzie's lap and whisper an idea for a movie into My Secret Agent Lover Man's ear. An idea to make him breathe deeply and sleep peacefully so the dark circles would fade from beneath his eyes. She wanted Weetzie and My Secret Agent Lover Man to stroke her hair and take her picture as if they were her real parents. But she did not go to them.

She turned to see Weetzie's mother, Brandy-Lynn, waltzing alone.

Weetzie had told Witch Baby that Brandy-Lynn had once been a beautiful starlet, and in the soft shadows of night roses, Witch Baby could see it now. Starlet. Starlit, like Weetzie and Cherokee, Witch Baby thought. Brandy-Lynn collapsed in a lawn chair to drink her martini and finger the silver heart locket she always wore around her neck. Inside the locket was a photograph of Weetzie's father, Charlie Bat, who had died years before. The white lights shone on the heart, the martini and the tears that slid down Brandy-Lynn's cheeks. Witch Baby wanted to pat the tears with her fingertip and taste the salt. Even after all this time, Brandy-Lynn cried often about Charlie Bat, but Witch Baby never cried about anything. Sometimes tears gathered, thick and seething salt in her chest, but she kept them there.

As Witch Baby imagined the way Brandy-Lynn's tears would feel on her own face, she saw Cherokee Bat dancing over to Brandy-Lynn and holding a piece of plantain pie.

"Eat some pie and come dance with me and Raphael, Grandma Brandy," Cherokee said. "You can show us how you danced when you were a movie star."

Brandy-Lynn wiped away her mascara-tinted tears and shakily held out her arms. Then she and Cherokee waltzed away across the lawn.

No one noticed Witch Baby as she went back

inside the cottage, into the room she and Cherokee shared.

Cherokee's side of the room was filled with feathers, crystals, butterfly wings, rocks, shells and dried flowers. There was a small tepee that Coyote had helped Cherokee make. The walls on Witch Baby's side of the room were covered with newspaper clippings—nuclear accidents, violence, poverty and disease. Every night, before she went to bed, Witch Baby cut out three articles or pictures with a pair of toenail scissors and taped them to the wall. They made Cherokee cry.

"Why do you want to have those up there?" Weetzie asked. "You'll both have nightmares."

If Witch Baby didn't cut out three articles, she knew she would lie awake, watching the darkness break up into grainy dots around her head like an enlarged newspaper photo.

Tonight, when she came to the third article, Witch Baby held her breath. Some Indians in South America had found a glowing blue ball. They stroked it, peeled off layers to decorate their walls and doorways, faces and bodies.

Then one day they began to die. All of them. The blue globe was the radioactive part of an old X-ray machine.

Witch Baby burrowed under her blankets as Brandy-Lynn, Weetzie and Cherokee entered the room with plates of food. In their feathers, flowers and fringe, with their starlit hair, they looked more like three sisters than grandmother, mother and daughter.

"There you are!" Weetzie said. "Have some Love-Rice and come dance with us, my baby witch."

Witch Baby peeked out at the three blondes and snarled at them.

"Are you looking for those articles again? Why do you need those awful things?" Brandy-Lynn asked.

"What time are we upon and where do I belong?" Witch Baby mumbled.

"You belong here. In this city. In this house. With all of us," said Weetzie.

Witch Baby scowled at the clippings on her wall. The pictures stared back—missing children smiling, not knowing what was going to happen to them later; serial killers looking blind also, in another way.

"Why is this place called Los Angeles?" Witch Baby asked. "There aren't any angels."

"Maybe there are. Sometimes I see angels in the people I love," said Weetzie.

"What do angels look like?"

"They have wings and carry lilies," Cherokee said. "And they have blonde hair," she added, tossing her braids.

"Clutch pig!" said Witch Baby under her breath. She tugged at her own dark tangles.

"No, Cherokee," said Weetzie. "That's just in some old paintings. Angels can look like anyone. They can look like mysterious, beautiful, purple-eyed girls. Now eat your rice, Witch Baby, and come outside with us."

But Witch Baby curled up like a snail.

"Please, Witch. Come out and dance."

Witch Baby snailed up tighter.

"All right, then, sleep well, honey-honey. Dream of your own angels," said Weetzie, kissing the top of her almost-daughter's head. "But remember, this is where you belong."

She took Cherokee's hand, linked arms with Brandy-Lynn and left the room.

❤

Witch Baby, who is not one of them, dreams of her own angel again. He is huddling on the curb of a dark, rainy street. Behind him is a building filled with golden lights, people and laughter, but he never goes inside. He stays out in the rain, the hollows of his eyes and cheeks full of shadows. When he sees Witch Baby, he opens his hands and holds them out to her. She never touches him in the dream, but she knows just how he would feel.

❤

Witch Baby got out of bed. She put the article about the radioactive ball into her pocket. She put her black cowboy-boot roller skates on her feet.

As she skated away from the cottage, Witch Baby thought of the blue people, dying and beautiful.

Devil City, she said to herself. Los Diablos.

Globe Lamp

Witch Baby passed the Charlie Chaplin Theater that had been shut down a long time ago and was covered with graffiti now. The theater still had pictures of Charlie Chaplin on the walls, and they reminded Witch Baby of My Secret Agent Lover Man.

Someday me and My Secret will reopen this theater, she thought. And we'll make our own movies together, movies that change things.

Witch Baby passed Canter's, the all-night coffee shop, where a man with dirt-blackened feet and a cloak of rags sat on the sidewalk sniffing pancakes in the air. She only had fifty cents in her pocket, but she placed it carefully in his palm, then skated on past the rows of markets that sold fruits and vegetables, almonds and raisins, olive oil and honey. The markets were all closed for the night. So was the shop where Weetzie always bought vanilla and Vienna coffee beans. But next to the coffee bean shop was a window filled with strange things. There were cupids, monster heads, mermaids, Egyptian cats, jaguars with clocks in their bellies, animal skulls; and lighting up all the rest was a lamp shaped like a globe of the world.

Witch Baby stood in front of the dust-streaked window, wondering why she had never noticed this place before. She stared at the globe, thinking of My Secret Agent Lover Man and the lamp he had told Weetzie about.

Then she opened the door and skated into a room cluttered with merry-go-round horses, broken china, bolts of glittery fabric, Persian carpets and many lamps. The lamps weren't lit and the room was so dark that Witch Baby could hardly see. But she did notice a gold turban rising just above a low counter at the back of the store. A humming voice came from beneath the turban.

"Greetings. What have you come for?" The voice was like an insect buzzing toward Witch Baby and she saw a pair of slanted firefly eyes watching her. A tiny man stepped from behind the counter. He smelled of almonds and smoke.

"I want the globe lamp," Witch Baby said.

The man shuffled closer. "My, my, I haven't seen one of my own kind in ages. You're certainly small enough and you have the eyes. But I wouldn't have recognized you in those rolling boots. Is that what we're wearing these days?" He looked down at his embroidered, pointed-toed slippers. "What have you come for?"

"The globe lamp," Witch Baby repeated.

"I wouldn't recommend the globe lamp. It's

not a traditional enough abode. On the other hand, you may not want to be bothered with all those people rubbing the lid and whispering their wishes all the time. It gets tiresome, doesn't it, this lamp business? They don't understand that the really good wishes like world peace are just out of our league and those love wishes are such a risk. So the globe's a fine disguise, I suppose. No one bothering you for happily ever after. I understand, believe me; that's why I quit. The lamp business I'm in now is much less complicated."

"What time are we upon and where do I belong?" Witch Baby asked.

"This is the time we're upon." He blinked three times, shuffled over to the window, drew back a black curtain and reached to touch the globe lamp. Suddenly it changed. Where there had been a painted sea, Witch Baby saw real water rippling. Where there had been painted continents, there were now forests, deserts and tiny, flickering cities. Witch Baby thought she heard a whisper of tears and moans, of gunshots and music.

The man unplugged the lamp, and it became

dark and still. He carried it over to Witch Baby and placed it in her arms. Because she was so small, the lamp hid everything except for two hands with bitten fingernails and two skinny legs in black cowboy-boot roller skates.

"Where do I belong?"

"At home," said the man. "At home in the globe."

When Witch Baby peeked around the globe lamp to thank him, she found herself standing on the sidewalk in front of a deserted building. There was only dust and shadow in the window, but somehow Witch Baby thought she saw the image of a tiny man reflected there. Skating home, she remembered the lights and whispers of the world.

It was late when Witch Baby returned to the cottage and tiptoed into the pink room that Weetzie and My Secret Agent Lover Man shared. They lay in their bed asleep, surrounded by bass guitars, tiki heads, balloons, two surfboards, a unicycle, a home-movie camera and Rubber Chicken. My Secret Agent Lover Man was tossing and turning and grinding his teeth. Weetzie lay beside him with her blonde mop of hair and aqua feather nightie. She was trying to stroke the lines out of his face.

Witch Baby watched them for a while. Then she plugged in the globe lamp, took the article about the glowing blue ball out of her pocket, put it on My Secret Agent Lover Man's chest and stepped back into the darkness.

Suddenly My Secret Agent Lover Man sat straight up in bed. He shone with sweat, blue in the globe-lamp light.

"What's wrong, honey-honey?" Weetzie asked, sitting up beside him and taking him in her arms.

"I dreamed about them again."

"The bodies . . . ?"

"Exploding. The men with masks."

"You'll feel better when you start your next movie," Weetzie said, rubbing his neck and shoulders and running her fingers through his hair. "You and our Witch Baby are just the same."

My Secret Agent Lover Man turned and saw the globe lamp shining in a corner of the room.

"Weetz!" he said. "Where did you find it?

· 18 ·

What a slinkster-cool gift! It's just like one I had when I was a kid."

"What are you talking about?" Weetzie asked. Then she turned, too, and saw the lamp. "Lanky Lizards!" she said. "I don't know where it came from!"

Witch Baby wanted to jump onto the bed, throw back her arms and say, "I know!" But instead she just watched. My Secret Agent Lover Man, who didn't look at all like Witch Baby now, stared as if he were hypnotized. Then he noticed the article, which had slipped into his lap.

"Two glowing blue globes," he said, gazing from the piece of paper to the lamp. "I'm going to make a new movie, Weetz. One that really says something. Thank you for your inspiration, my magic slink!"

Before she could speak he took her in his arms and pressed his lips to hers.

Witch Baby turned away. Although her walls were papered with other pieces of pain, although her eyes were globes, he had not recognized her gift. She did not belong here.

Drum Love

In the garden shed, behind a cobweb curtain, Witch Baby was playing her drums. It was the drumming of flashing dinosaur rock gods and goddesses who sweat starlight, the drumming of tall, muscly witch doctors who can make animals dance, wounds heal, rain fall and flowers open. But it began in Witch Baby's head and heart and came out through her small body and hands. Her only audience was a row of pictures she had taken of Raphael Chong Jah-Love.

Witch Baby had been in love with Raphael for as long as she could remember. His parents, Ping and Valentine, had known Weetzie even before she had met My Secret Agent Lover Man, and Raphael had played with Witch Baby and Cherokee since they were babies. Not only did Raphael look like powdered chocolate, but he smelled like it, too, and his eyes reminded Witch Baby of Hershey's Kisses. His mother, Ping, dressed him in bright red, green and yellow and twisted his hair into dreadlocks. ("Cables to heaven," said his father, Valentine, who had dreads too.) Raphael, the Chinese-Rasta parrot boy, loved to paint, and he covered the walls of his room with waterfalls, stars, rainbows, suns, moons, birds, flowers and fish. As soon as Witch Baby had learned to walk, she had chased after him, spying and dreaming that someday they would roll in the mud, dance with paint on their feet and play music together while Cherokee Bat took photographs of them.

But Raphael never paid much attention to Witch Baby. Until the day he came into the garden shed and stood staring at her with his slanted chocolate-Kiss eyes.

Witch Baby stopped drumming with her hands, but her heart began to pound. She didn't want Raphael to see the pictures of himself. "Go away!" she said.

He looked far into her pupils, then turned and left the shed. Witch Baby beat hard on the drums to keep her tears from coming.

Witch babies never cry, she told herself.

The next day Raphael came back to the shed. Witch Baby stopped drumming and snarled at him.

"How did you get so good?" he asked her.

"I taught myself."

"You taught yourself! How?"

"I just hear it in my head and feel it in my hands."

"But what got you started? What made you want to play?"

Witch Baby remembered the day My Secret

Agent Lover Man had brought her the drum set. She had pretended she wasn't interested because she was afraid that Cherokee would try to use the drums too. Then she had hidden them in the garden shed, soundproofed the walls with foam and shag carpeting, put on her favorite records and taught herself to play. No one had ever heard her except for the flower-pots, the cobwebs, the pictures of Raphael and, now, Raphael himself.

"When I play drums I don't need to bite or kick or break, steal Duck's Fig Newtons or tear the hair off Cherokee's Kachina Barbies," Witch Baby whispered.

"Teach me," Raphael said.

Witch Baby gnawed on the end of the drum-stick.

"Teach me to play drums."

She narrowed her eyes.

"There is a girl I know," Raphael said, look-ing at Witch Baby. "And she would be very happy if I learned."

Witch Baby couldn't remember how to breathe. She wasn't sure if you take air in through your nose and let it out through your mouth or the other way around. There was only one girl, she thought, who would be very happy if Raphael learned to play drums, so happy that her toes would uncurl and her heart would play music like a magic bongo drum.

Witch Baby looked down at the floor of the shed so her long eyelashes, that had a purple tint from the reflection of her eyes, fanned out across the top of her cheeks. She held the drumsticks out to Raphael.

From then on, Raphael came over all the time for his lessons. He wasn't a very good drummer, but he looked good, biting his lip, raising his eyebrows and moving his neck back and forth so his dreadlocks danced. For Witch Baby, the best part of the lessons was when she got to play for him. He recorded her on tape and never took his eyes off her. It was as if she were being seen by someone for the first time. She imagined that the music turned into stars and birds and fish, like the ones Raphael painted, and spun, floated, swam in the air around them.

One day Raphael asked Witch Baby if he

could play a tape he had made of her drumming and follow along silently, gesturing as if he were really playing.

"That way I'll feel like I'm as good as you, and I'll be more brave when I play," he said.

Witch Baby put on the tape and Raphael drummed along silently in the air.

Then the door of the shed opened, and Cherokee came in, brushing cobwebs out of her way. She was wearing her white suede fringed minidress and her moccasins, and she had feathers and turquoise beads in her long pale hair. Standing in the dim shed, Cherokee glowed. Raphael looked up while he was drumming and his chocolate-Kiss eyes seemed to melt. Witch Baby glared at Cherokee through a snarl of hair and chewed her nails.

Cherokee Brat Bath Mat Bat, she thought. Clutch pig! Go away and leave us alone. You do not belong here.

But Cherokee was lost in the music and began to dance, stamping and whirling like a small blonde Indian. She left trails of light in the air, and Raphael watched as if he were trying to paint pictures of her in his mind.

When the song was over, Cherokee went to Raphael and kissed him on the cheek.

"You are a slink-chunk, slam-dunk drummer, Raphael. I didn't really care about you learning to play drums. I just wanted to see what you'd do for me—how hard you'd try to be my best friend. But you've turned into a love-drum, drum-love!"

"Cherokee," he said softly.

She took his hand and they left the shed.

Witch Baby's heart felt like a giant bee sting, like a bee had stung her inside where her heart was supposed to be. Every time she heard her own drumbeats echoing in her head, the sting swelled with poison. She threw herself against the drums, kicking and clawing until she was bruised and some of the drumskins were torn. Then she curled up on the floor of the shed, among the cobwebs that Cherokee had ruined, reminding herself that witch babies do not cry.

After that day Raphael Chong Jah-Love and Cherokee Bat became inseparable. They hiked up canyon trails, collected pebbles, looked for deer, built fires, had powwows, made papooses out of puppies and lay warming their bellies on rocks and chanting to the animals, trees, and earth, "You are all my relations," the way My Secret Agent Lover Man's friend Coyote had showed them. They painted on every surface they could find, including each other. They spent hours gazing at each other until their eyes were all pupil and Cherokee's looked as dark as Raphael's. No one could get their attention.

Weetzie, My Secret Agent Lover Man, and Valentine and Ping Chong Jah-Love watched them.

"They are just babies still," My Secret Agent Lover Man said. "How could they be so in love? They remind me of us."

"If I had met you when I was little, I would have acted the same way," Weetzie said.

"But it's funny," said Ping. "I always thought *Witch Baby* was secretly in love with Raphael."

While Raphael and Cherokee fell in love, they forgot all about drums. Witch Baby stopped playing drums too. She pulled apart Cherokee's Kachina Barbie dolls, scattering their limbs throughout the cottage and even sticking some parts in Brandy-Lynn's Jell-O mold. She stole Duck's Fig Newtons, made dresses out of Dirk's best shirts and bit Weetzie's fingers when Weetzie tried to serve her vegetables.

"Witch Baby! Stop that! Weetzie's fingers are not carrots!" My Secret Agent Lover Man exclaimed, kissing Weetzie's nibbled fingertips.

Witch Baby went around the cottage taking candid pictures of everyone looking their worst—My Secret Agent Lover Man with a hangover, Weetzie covered with paint and glue, Dirk and Duck arguing, Brandy-Lynn weeping into a martini, Cherokee and Raphael gobbling up the vegetarian lasagna Weetzie was saving for dinner.

Witch Baby was wild, snarled, tangled and angry. Everyone got more and more frustrated with her. When they tried to grab her, even for a hug, she would wriggle away, her body quick-slippery as a fish. She never cried, but she always wanted to cry. Finally, while she was watching Cherokee and Raphael running around the cottage in circles, whooping and flapping their feather-decorated arms, Witch Baby remembered something Cherokee had done to her when they were very young. Late at night she got out of her bed, took the toenail scissors she had hidden under her pillow, crept over to Cherokee's tepee and snipped at Cherokee's hair. She did not cut straight across, but chopped unevenly, and the ragged strands of hair fell like moonlight.

The next morning Witch Baby hid in the shed and waited. Then she heard a scream coming from the cottage. She felt as if someone had crammed a bean-cheese-hot-dog-pastrami burrito down her throat.

Witch Baby hid in the shed all day. When everyone was asleep she crept back into the cottage, went into the violet-and-aqua-tiled bathroom and stared at herself in the mirror. She saw a messy nest of hair, a pale, skinny body, knobby, skinned knees and feet with curling toes.

No wonder Raphael doesn't love me, Witch Baby thought. I am a baby witch.

She took the toenail scissors and began to chop at her own hair. Then she plugged in My

Secret Agent Lover Man's razor, turned it on and listened to it buzz at her like a hungry metal animal.

When her scalp was completely bald, Witch Baby, with her deep-set, luminous, jacaranda-blossom-colored eyes, looked as if she had drifted down from some other planet.

But Witch Baby did not see her eerie, fairy, genie, moon-witch beauty, the beauty of twilight and rainstorms. "You'll never belong to anyone," she said to the bald girl in the mirror.

Tree Spirit

The chain saws were buzzing like giant razors. Witch Baby pressed her palms over her ears.

"What is going on?" Coyote cried, padding into the cottage.

Witch Baby had hardly ever heard Coyote raise his voice before. She curled up under the clock, and he knelt beside her so that his long braid brushed her cheek. She saw the full veins in his callused hands, the turquoise-studded band, blood-blue, at his wrist.

"Where is everyone, my little bald one?" he asked gently.

"They went to the street fair."

"And they left you here with the dying trees?"

"I didn't want to go with them."

Coyote put his hand on Witch Baby's head. It fit perfectly like a cap. His touch quieted the saws for a moment and stilled the blood beating at Witch Baby's naked temples. "Why not?" he asked.

"I get lonely with them."

"With all that big family you have?"

"More than when I'm alone."

Coyote nodded. "I would rather be alone most of the time. It's quieter. Someday I will live in the desert again with the Joshua trees." He took a handkerchief out of his leather backpack and unfolded it. Inside were five seeds. "Joshua tree seeds," he said. "In the blue desert moonlight, if you put your arms around Joshua trees and are very quiet, you can hear them speaking to you. Sometimes, if you turn around fast enough, you can catch them dancing behind your back."

Coyote squinted out the window at the falling branches, the whirlwind of leaves, blossoms and dust.

"Now I'm going to do something about those tree murderers." He went to the phone book, found the number of the school across the street, and called.

"I need to speak to the principal. It's about the trees."

He waited, drumming his fingers. Witch Baby crept up beside him, peering over the tabletop at the sunset desert of his face.

"Is this the principal? I'd like to ask you why you are cutting those trees down. I would think that a school would be especially concerned. Do you know how long it takes trees to grow? Especially in this foul air?"

The saws kept buzzing brutally while he spoke. Witch Baby thought about the jacaranda trees across the street. Coyote had told her that all trees have spirits, and she imagined women with long, light-boned limbs and falls of whispery green hair, dark Coyote men with skin like clay as it smooths on the potter's wheel. Some might even be hairless girls like Witch Baby—the purple-eyed spirits of jacaranda trees.

Finally, Coyote put the phone down. He and Witch Baby sat together at the window, wincing as all the trees in front of the school became a woodpile scattered with purple blossoms.

Coyote is like My Secret and me, Witch Baby thought, feeling the warmth of his presence beside her. But he recognizes that I am like him and My Secret doesn't see.

Witch Baby's almost-family came home and saw them still sitting there. Weetzie invited Coyote to stay for dinner but he solemnly shook his head.

"I couldn't eat anything after what we saw today," he said.

That night, when everyone else was asleep, Witch Baby unfolded the handkerchief she had stolen from Coyote's backpack and looked at the five Joshua tree seeds. They seemed to glow, and she thought she heard them whispering as she crept out the window and into the moonlight. In the soil from which the jacaranda trees had been torn, Witch Baby knelt and planted Coyote's five seeds, imagining how one day she and Coyote would fling their arms around five Joshua trees. If she was very quiet she might be able to hear the trees telling her the secrets of the desert.

♥

"Where are they?"

Coyote stood towering above Witch Baby's bed. She blinked up at him, her dreams of singing trees passing away like clouds across the moon, until she saw his face clearly. His hair was unbraided and fell loose around his shoulders.

"Where are my Joshua tree seeds, Witch Baby?"

Witch Baby sat up in bed. It was early morning and still quiet. There was no buzzing today; all the trees were already down.

"I planted them for you," she said.

Coyote looked as if the sound of chain saws were still filling his head. "What? You planted them? Where did you plant them? Those were special seeds. My Secret Agent Lover Man brought them to me from the desert. I told him I had to take them back the next time I went, because Joshua trees grow only on sacred desert ground. They'll never grow where you planted them."

"But I planted them in front of the school because of yesterday. They'll grow there and we'll always be able to look at them and listen to what they tell us."

"They'll never grow," Coyote said. "They are lost."

Witch Baby spent the next three nights clutching a flashlight and digging in the earth in front of the school for the Joshua tree seeds, but there was no sign of them. Her fingers ached, the nails full of soil, the knuckles scratched by rocks and twigs. She was kneeling in dirt, covered in dirt, wishing for the tree spirits to take her away with them to a place where Joshua trees sang and danced in the blue moonlight.

Stowawitch

It was Dirk who found Witch Baby digging in the dirt. He was taking a late-night run on his glowing silver Nikes when he noticed the spot of light flitting over the ground in front of the school. Then he saw the outline of a tree spirit crouched in the darkness. He ran over and called to Witch Baby.

"What are you doing out here, Miss Witch?"

Witch Baby flicked off the flashlight and didn't answer, but when Dirk came over, she let him lift her in his beautiful, sweaty arms and carry her into the house. She leaned against him, limp with exhaustion.

"Never go off at night by yourself anymore," Dirk said as he tucked her into bed. "If you want, you can wake me and we can go on a run. I know what it's like to feel scared and awake in the night. Sometimes I could go dig in the earth too, when I feel that way."

Before Witch Baby fell asleep that night she looked at the picture she had taken of Dirk and Duck at the party. Dirk, who looked even taller than he was because of his Mohawk and thick-soled creepers, was pretending to balance a champagne glass on Duck's flat-top and Duck's blue eyes were rolled upward, watching the glass. Almost anyone could see by the picture that Dirk and Duck were in love.

Dirk and Duck are different from most people too, Witch Baby thought. Sometimes they must feel like they don't belong just because they love each other.

When Dirk and Duck announced that they were going to Santa Cruz to visit Duck's family, Witch Baby asked if she could go with them.

"I'm sorry, Witch Baby," Dirk said, rubbing his hand over the fuzz that had grown back on her scalp. "Duck and I need to spend some time alone together. Someday, when you are in love, you will understand."

"Besides, I haven't seen my family in years," Duck said. "It might be kind of an intense scene. We'll bring you back some mini-Birkenstock sandals from Santa Cruz, though."

But Witch Baby didn't want Birkenstocks. And she already understood about spending time with the person you love. She wanted to go to Santa Cruz with Dirk and Duck, especially since she could never go anywhere with Raphael.

I'll be a stowaway, Witch Baby thought.

Dirk and Duck put their matching surfboards, their black-and-yellow wet suits, their flannel shirts, long underwear, Guatemalan shorts, hooded mole-man sweatshirts, Levi's and Vans and Weetzie's avocado sandwiches into Dirk's red 1955 Pontiac, Jerry, and kissed everyone good-bye—everyone except for Witch Baby, who had disappeared.

"I hope she's okay," Weetzie said.

"She's just hiding," said My Secret Agent Lover Man.

"Give the witch child these." Duck handed Weetzie a fresh box of Fig Newtons. He did not know that Witch Baby was hidden in Jerry's trunk, eating the rest of the Newtons he had packed away there.

On the way to Santa Cruz Dirk and Duck stopped along the coast to surf. They stopped so many times to surf and eat (they finished the avocado sandwiches in the first fifteen minutes and bought sunflower seeds, licorice, peaches and Foster's Freeze soft ice cream along the way) that they didn't get to Santa Cruz until late that night. Duck was driving when they arrived, and he pulled Jerry up in front of the Drake house where Duck's mother, Darlene, lived with her boyfriend, Chuck, and Duck's eight brothers and sisters. It was an old house, painted white, with a tangled garden and a bay window full of lace and crystals. In the driveway was a Volvo station wagon with a "Visualize World Peace" bumper sticker.

Dirk and Duck sat there in the dark car, and neither of them said anything for a long time. Witch Baby peeked out from the trunk and imagined Duck playing in the garden as a little Duck, freckled and tan. She imagined a young Duck running out the front door in a yellow wet suit with a too-big surfboard under one arm and flippers on his feet.

"I wish I could tell my mom about us," Duck said to Dirk, "but she'll never understand. I think we should wait till morning to go in. I don't want to wake them."

"Whatever you need to do," Dirk said. "We can go to a motel or sleep in Jerry."

"I have a better idea," said Duck.

That night they slept on a picnic table at the beach, wrapped in sweaters and blankets to keep them warm. Duck looked at the full moon and said to Dirk, "The moon reminds me of my mom. So does the sound of the ocean. She used to say, 'Duck, how do you see the moon? Duck, how do you hear the ocean?' I can't remember how I used to answer."

When Dirk and Duck were asleep, Witch Baby climbed out of the trunk, stretched and peed.

I wish I could play my drums so they sounded the way I hear the ocean, she thought, closing her eyes and trying to fill herself with the concert of the night.

Then she looked up at the moon.

How do I see the moon? I wish I had a real mother to ask me.

The next morning, while Witch Baby hid in Jerry's trunk, Dirk and Duck hugged each other, surfed, took showers at the beach, put on clean clothes, slicked back their hair, hugged each other and drove to the Drake house.

Some children with upturned noses and blonde hair like Duck's and Birkenstocks on their feet were playing with three white dogs in the garden. When Dirk and Duck came up the path, one of the children screamed, "Duck!" All of them ran and jumped on him, covering him with kisses. Then three older children came out of the house and jumped on Duck too.

"Dirk, this is Peace, Granola, Crystal, Chi, Aura, Tahini and the twins, Yin and Yang," Duck said. "Everybody, this is my friend, Dirk McDonald."

A petite blonde woman wearing Birkenstocks and a sundress came out of the house. "Duck!" she cried. "Duck!" She ran to him and they embraced.

Witch Baby watched from the trunk.

"We have missed you so much," Darlene Drake said. "Well, come in, come inside. Have some pancakes. Chuck'll be home soon."

Duck looked at Dirk. Then he said, "Mom, this is my friend, Dirk McDonald."

"I'm very happy to meet you, Mrs. Drake," Dirk said, putting out his hand.

"Hi, Dirk," said Darlene, but she hardly glanced at him. She was staring at her oldest son. "You look more like your dad than ever," she said, and her eyes filled with tears. "I wish he could see you!"

Dirk, Duck, Darlene and the little Drakes

went into the house. Witch Baby climbed out of Jerry's trunk and sat in the flower box, watching through the window. She saw Darlene serve Duck and Dirk whole-wheat pancakes full of bananas and pecans and topped with plain yogurt and maple syrup. A little later the kitchen door opened and a big man with a red face came in.

"Chuck, honey, look who's here!" Darlene said, scurrying to him.

"Well, look who decided to wander back in!" Chuck said in a deep voice. He started to laugh. "Hey, Duck-dude! We thought you drowned or something, man!"

"Chuck!" said Darlene.

Duck looked at his pancakes.

"I'm just glad he's here now," Darlene said. "And this is Duck's friend . . ."

"Dirk," Dirk said.

"Do you surf, Dirk?" Chuck asked.

"Yes."

"Well, me, you and Duck can catch some Santa Cruz waves. And I'll show you where the No-Cal babes hang," Chuck said.

"Chuck!" said Darlene.

"Darlene hates that," Chuck said, pinching her.

"Stop it, Chuck," Darlene said.

Witch Baby took a photograph of Duck pushing his pancakes around in a pool of syrup while Dirk glanced from him to Chuck and back. Then she climbed in through the window, hopping onto a plate of pancakes on the kitchen table.

"Oh my!" Darlene gasped. "Who is this?"

"Witch Baby!" Dirk and Duck shouted. "How did you get here?"

"I stowed away."

"I better call home and tell them," Duck said. "They're probably going crazy trying to find you." He got up to use the phone.

"Oh, you're a friend of Duck's," Darlene said as Duck left the room. "Well, stop dancing on the pancakes. You must be hungry; you're so skinny." She pointed at Witch Baby's black high-top sneakers covered with rubber bugs. "And we should get you some nice sandals."

Witch Baby thought of her toes curling out of a pair of Birkenstocks and looked down at the floor.

"They were worried about you, Witch Child," Duck said when he came back. "Weetzie bit off all her fingernails and My Secret Agent Lover Man drove around looking for you all night. Never run away like that again!"

Did they really miss me? she wondered. Did they even know who it was who was gone?

Duck turned to his brothers and sisters, who were staring at Witch Baby with their identical sets of blue eyes. "This is my family, Peace, Granola, Crystal, Chi, Aura, Tahini and Yin and Yang Drake," Duck said. "You guys, this is Witch Baby. She's my . . . she's our . . . well, she's our pancake dancer stowawitch!"

Witch Baby bared her teeth and Yin and Yang giggled. Then all Duck's brothers and sisters ran off to play in the garden.

Duck Mother

In Santa Cruz, Dirk, Duck and Darlene went for walks on the beach, hiked in the redwoods, marketed for organic vegetables and tofu and fed the chickens, the goat and the rabbit. Witch Baby followed along, taking pictures, whistling, growling, doing cartwheels, flips and imitations of Rubber Chicken and

Charlie Chaplin and throwing pebbles at Dirk, Duck and Darlene when they ignored her. Sometimes, when a pebble skimmed her head, Darlene would turn around, look at the girl with the fuzzy scalp and sigh.

"Where did you find her?" she said to Dirk. "I've never seen a child like that." Then she would link arms with Duck and Dirk and keep walking.

"Mom, don't say that so loud!" Duck would say. "You'll hurt her feelings."

But Witch Baby had already heard. She poked her tongue out at Darlene and tossed another pebble.

Clutch mother duck!

That evening, Dirk, Duck and Darlene were walking the dogs. Witch Baby was following them, watching and listening and sniffing the sea and pine in the air.

"Dirk, you are such a gentleman," Darlene said. "Your parents did a good job of raising you."

"I was raised by my Grandma Fifi," Dirk said. "My parents died when I was really little.

I don't even remember them. They were both killed in a car accident."

Darlene's eyes filled with tears. "Like Duck's dad," she said.

That night she gave both Dirk and Duck fisherman sweaters that had belonged to Duck's dad, Eddie Drake. She didn't give Witch Baby anything.

Witch Baby kept watching and listening and nibbling her fingernails. She hid in the closet in Duck's old bedroom, with the fading surf pictures on the walls and the twin beds with surfing Snoopy sheets, and heard Duck and Dirk talking about Darlene's boyfriend, Chuck.

"He is such a greaseburger!" Duck told Dirk.

"Tell me about your dad, Duck," Dirk said. He had asked before, but Duck wouldn't talk about Eddie Drake.

"He was a killer Malibu surfer," Duck said. "I mean, a *fine* athlete. He had this real peaceful look on his face, a little spaced out, you know, but at peace. They were totally in love.

She was Miss Zuma Beach. They fell in love when they were fourteen and, like, that was it. They had all of us one right after the other. Me while they were into the total surf scene when we lived in Malibu, Peace and Granola during their hippie-rebel phase, and then they got more into Eastern philosophy—you know, the twins, Yin and Yang. But then he died. He was surfing." Duck blinked the tears out of his eyes. "I still can't talk about it," he said.

"Duck." Dirk touched his cheek.

"I remember, later, my mom trying to run into the water and I'm trying to hold her back and her hair and my tears are so bright that I'm blind. I knew she would have walked right into the ocean after him and kept going. In a way I wanted to go too."

"Don't say that, puppy," Dirk whispered.

Witch Baby tried to swallow the sandy lump in her throat.

"But who the hell is Chuck?" Duck said. "I couldn't believe she'd be with a greaseburger like that, so I left. Plus, I knew they'd never understand about me liking guys."

Dirk kissed a tear that had slid onto Duck's tan and freckled shoulder and he drew Duck into his arms, into arms that had lifted Witch Baby from the dirt the night she had been searching for the Joshua tree seeds.

Just then, Witch Baby stepped out of the closet, holding out her finger to touch Duck's tears, wanting to share Dirk's arms.

"What are you doing here, Witch?" Duck said, startled.

"Go back to bed, Witch Baby," said Dirk, and she scampered away.

Later, curled beneath the cot that Darlene had set up for her in Yin and Yang's room, Witch Baby tried to think of ways to make Dirk and Duck see that she understood them, she understood them better than anyone, even better than Duck's own mother. Then they might let her stay with them and see their tears, she thought.

The next day Duck and Darlene were walking through the redwood forest. Witch Baby was following them.

"Duck!" Witch Baby called, "Do you know

that all trees have spirits? Maybe your dad is a tree now! Maybe your dad is a tree or a wave!"

Duck glanced at Darlene, concerned, then turned to Witch Baby and put his finger on his lips. "Let's talk about that later, Witch. Go and play with the twins or something," he said, and kept walking.

"Duck, why did you go away?" Darlene asked, ignoring Witch Baby. "What have you been doing with your life?"

Duck told Darlene about the cottage and his friends. He told her about the slinkster-cool movies they made, the jamming music they played and the dream waves they surfed. The Love-Rice fiestas, Chinese moon dragon celebrations and Jamaican beach parties.

"You sound very happy," Darlene said. "Do you have a girlfriend to take care of you?"

"My friends and I take care of each other," Duck said. "We are like a family."

"That's good," said Darlene. "They sound wonderful. The little witch is a little strange, but I really like Dirk."

Just then Witch Baby jumped down on the path in front of Duck and Darlene. She was covered with leaves and grimacing like an angry tree imp.

"That's good," she said. "That you like Dirk. Because Duck likes Dirk a lot too. They love each other more than anyone else in the world. They even sleep in the same bed with their arms around each other!"

"Witch Child!" Duck tried to grab her arm, but he missed and she escaped up into the branches of a young redwood.

Darlene stood absolutely still. The light through the ferns made her blonde hair turn a soft green. She looked at Duck.

"What does she mean?" Darlene asked. And then she began to cry.

She cried and cried. Duck put his arms around her, but no matter what Duck said, Darlene kept crying. She cried the whole way along the redwood path to the car. She cried the whole way back to the house, never saying a word.

"Mom!" Duck said. "Please, Mom. Talk to me! Why are you crying so much? I'm still me. I'm still here."

Darlene kept crying.

Back at the house Chuck was barbecuing burgers. Dirk and the kids were playing softball.

"What is it, Darlene?" Chuck asked.

Darlene just kept crying. Dirk came and stood next to Duck.

"I'm gay," Duck said suddenly.

Chuck and all Duck's brothers and sisters stared. Even Darlene's sobs quieted. Dirk raised his eyebrows in surprise. Duck's voice had sounded so strong and clear and sure.

There was a long silence.

"Better take a life insurance policy out on you!" Chuck said, laughing. "The way things are these days."

"Chuck!" Darlene began to sob again.

"You pretend to be so liberal and free and politically correct and you don't even try to understand," Duck said. "We're leaving."

"Clutch pigs!" said Witch Baby. "You can't even love your own son just because he loves Dirk. Dirk and Duck are the most slinkster-cool team."

Duck ran into the house to pack his things, and Dirk and Witch Baby followed him.

A little while later they all got into Jerry and began to drive away.

"Wait, Duck!" his brothers and sisters called. "Duck, wait, stay! Come back!"

Darlene hid her ex-Zuma-Beach-beauty-queen face in her hands. Chuck was flipping burgers. Dirk looked back as he drove Jerry away but Duck stared straight ahead. Witch Baby hid her head under a blanket.

On the way home from Santa Cruz, Dirk and Duck stopped to walk on the beach. They were wearing their matching hooded mole-man sweatshirts. Witch Baby walked a few feet behind them, hopping into their footprints, but they hardly noticed her. It was sunset and the sand looked pinkish silver.

"There are places somewhere in the world where colored sparks fly out of the sand," Dirk told Duck, trying to distract him. "And I've heard that right here, if you stare at the sun when it sets, you'll see a flash of green."

Duck was staring straight ahead at the pink clouds in the sky. There was a space in the clouds filled with deepening blue and one star.

"I want to let go of everything," Duck said.

"All the pain and fear. I want to let it float away through that space in the clouds. That is what the sky and water are saying to do. Don't hold on to anything. But I can't let go of these feelings."

"Let go of everything," Witch Baby murmured.

Dirk put his arms around Duck.

"How could she be with him?" Duck asked the sky.

"She must have been lonely," Dirk said.

"If I ever lost you, no amount of loneliness or anything could drive me into the arms of another!" Duck said. "Especially not into the arms of a greaseburger like Chuck!"

Witch Baby felt like burying herself head-first in the sand. She knew that if she did, Dirk would not lift her in his arms like a precious plant, as he had done that night in front of the school. She knew that Duck would never share his tears with her now.

Dirk and Duck gazed at the ocean.

"How do you hear the water?" Dirk asked Duck.

❤

Dirk and Duck and Witch Baby didn't arrive at the cottage for three days because they stopped to camp along the coast. The whole time Dirk and Duck ignored Witch Baby. She wished she had her drums to play for them so that they might understand what she felt inside.

When they got home, they smelled garlic, basil and oregano as they came in the door. They entered the dining room and Duck practically jumped out of his Vans. There at the table with Weetzie, My Secret Agent Lover Man, Cherokee and Raphael sat Darlene, Granola, Peace, Crystal, Chi, Aura, Tahini and Yin and Yang Drake.

Darlene didn't have tears in her eyes. She and Weetzie were leaning together over their candle-lit angel hair pasta and laughing.

"Duck!" Darlene leaped up and ran to him. "I need to talk to you."

Darlene and Duck went out onto the porch. The crickets chirped and there were stars in the sky. The air smelled of flowers, smog and dinners.

"Duck," Darlene said. "After you told me, I

went to everyone—my acupuncturist, my crystal healer and my sand-tray therapist. Then I went for a long walk and thought about you. I realized that it wasn't you so much as me, Duck. My femininity felt threatened. I don't know if you can understand that, but that's how it was. I felt that if my oldest son rejects women, he's rejecting me. That somehow I made him—you—feel bad about women. Ever since your dad died, I've been so vulnerable and confused about everything."

"This is crazy!" Duck said. "You are such a beautiful woman. And how I feel about Dirk has nothing to do with your femininity. I love Dirk. It just is that way."

"I don't understand," Darlene said. "But I'll try. I am worried about your health, though."

"Everyone has to be careful," Duck said. "Dirk and I believe there will be a cure very soon. But we are safe that way, now."

"I love you, Duck," said Darlene. "And your friend Dirk is darling. Your father would be proud of you."

"I miss him so much," said Duck putting his

arms around her. "But he's still guiding us in a way, you know? When I'm surfing, especially, I feel like he's with me."

Suddenly there was the click and flash of a camera and Duck turned to see Witch Baby photographing them.

A few days later, after Darlene and the little Drakes had left, Duck found a new photograph pasted on the moon clock. The picture on the number eleven showed Weetzie, My Secret Agent Lover Man, Dirk, Duck, Cherokee, Raphael, Valentine, Ping, Coyote, Brandy-Lynn and Darlene. Their arms were linked and they were all smiling, cheese. It looked as if everyone except Witch Baby were having a picnic on the moon.

Angel Wish

No one at the cottage paid much attention to Witch Baby when she got back from Santa Cruz. They didn't even mention how worried they had been when she had disappeared. Everyone was too busy working on My Secret Agent Lover Man's new movie, *Los Diablos*, about the glowing blue radioactive ball.

So Witch Baby skated to the Spanish bungalow where Valentine and Ping Chong Jah-Love
lived. Raphael lived with them, but he was almost always at the cottage with Cherokee.

Wind chimes hung like glass leaves from the
porch, and the rosebush Ping had planted
bloomed different colored roses on Valentine's,
Ping's and Raphael's birthdays—one rose for
each year. Now there were white roses for
Ping. Inside, the bungalow was like a miniature rain forest. Valentine's wood carvings
of birds and ebony people peered out among
the ferns and small potted trees. Ping's shim-
mering green weavings were draped from the
ceiling. Witch Baby sat in the Jah-Love rain
forest bungalow watching Ping with her bird-
of-paradise hair, kohl-lined eyes, coral lips,
batik sarong skirt and jade dragon pendants,
sewing a sapphire blue Chinese silk shirt for
Valentine.

"Baby Jah-Love," Ping Chong sang. "Why
are you so sad? Once I was sad like you. And
then I met Valentine in a rain forest in Jamaica. He appeared out of the green mist. I
had been dreaming of him and wishing for him

forever. When I met Valentine I wasn't afraid anymore. I knew that my soul would always have a reflection and an echo and that even if we were apart—and we were for a while in the beginning—I finally knew what my soul looked and sounded like. I would have that forever, like a mirror or an echoing canyon."

Ping stopped, seeing Witch Baby's eyes. She knew Witch Baby was thinking about Raphael.

"Sometimes our Jah-Love friends fool us," she said. "We think we've found them and then they're just not the one. They look right and sound right and play the right instrument, even, but they're just not who we are looking for. I thought I found Valentine three times before I really did. And then there he was in the forest, like a tree that had turned into a man."

Witch Baby wanted to ask Ping how to find her Jah-Love angel. She knew Raphael was not him, even though Raphael had the right eyes and smile and name. She knew how he looked—the angel in her dream—but she didn't know how to find him. Should she roller-skate through the streets in the evenings when the streetlights flicker on? Should she stow away to Jamaica on a cruise ship and search for him in the rain forests and along the beaches? Would he come to her? Was he waiting, dreaming of her in the same way she waited and dreamed? Witch Baby thought that if anyone could help, it would be Ping, with her quick, small hands that could create dresses out of anything and make hair look like bunches of flowers or garlands of serpents, cables to heaven. But Witch Baby didn't know how to ask.

"Wishes are the best way," said a deep voice. It was the voice of Valentine Jah-Love. He had been building a set for *Los Diablos* and had come home to eat a lunch of noodles and coconut milk shakes with Ping.

Valentine sat beside Ping, circling her with his sleek arm, and grinned down at Witch Baby. "Wish on everything. Pink cars are good, especially old ones. And stars of course, first stars and shooting stars. Planes will do if they are the first light in the sky and look like stars. Wish in tunnels, holding your breath and lifting your feet off the ground. Birthday candles. Baby teeth."

Valentine showed his teeth, which were bright as candles. Then he got up and slipped the sapphire silk shirt over his dark shoulders.

"Even if you get your wish, there are usually complications. I wished for Ping Chong, but I didn't know we'd have so many problems in the world, from our families and even the ones we thought were our friends, just because my skin is dark and she is the color of certain lilies. But still you must wish." He looked at Ping. "I think Witch Baby might just find her angel on the set of *Los Diablos*," he said, pulling a tiny pink Thunderbird out of his trouser pocket. It came rolling toward Witch Baby through the tunnel Valentine made with his hand.

Niña Bruja

On the set of *Los Diablos*, My Secret Agent Lover Man and Weetzie sat in their canvas chairs, watching a group of dark children gathered in a circle around a glowing blue ball. Valentine was putting some finishing touches on a hut he had built. Ping was painting some actors glossy blue. Dirk and Duck were in the office making phone calls and looking at photos.

Witch Baby went to the set of *Los Diablos* to hide costumes, break light bulbs and throw pebbles at everyone. That was when she saw Angel Juan Perez for the first time.

But it wasn't really the first time. Witch Baby had dreamed about Angel Juan before she ever saw him. He had been the dark angel boy in her dream.

When the real Angel Juan saw Witch Baby watching him from behind My Secret Agent Lover Man's director's chair, he did the same thing that the dream Angel Juan had done—he stretched out his arms and opened his hands. She sent Valentine's pink Thunderbird rolling toward his feet and ran away.

"Niña Bruja!" Angel Juan called. "I've heard about you. Come back here!"

But she was already gone.

The next day Witch Baby watched Angel Juan on the set again. Coyote was covering Angel Juan's face with blue shavings from the sacred ball. They sat in the dark and Angel Juan's blue face glowed.

When the scene was over, Angel Juan found Witch Baby hiding behind My Secret Agent Lover Man's chair again.

"Come with me, Niña Bruja," he said, holding out his hand.

Witch Baby crossed her arms on her chest and stuck out her chin. Angel Juan shrugged, but when he skateboarded away she followed him on her roller skates. Soon they were rolling along side by side on the way to the cottage.

They climbed up a jacaranda tree in the garden and sat in the branches until their hair was covered with purple blossoms; climbed down and slithered through the mud, pretending to be seeds. They sprayed each other with the hose, and the water caught sunlight so that they were rinsed in showers of liquid rainbows. In the house they ate banana and peanut butter sandwiches, put on music and pretended to surf on Witch Baby's bed under the newspaper clippings.

"Where are you from, Angel Juan?" Witch Baby asked.

"Mexico."

Witch Baby had seen sugar skulls and candelabras in the shapes of doves, angels and trees. She had seen white dresses embroidered with gardens, and she had seen paintings of a dark woman with parrots and flowers and blood and one eyebrow. She liked tortillas with butter melting in the fold almost as much as candy, and she liked hot days and hibiscus flowers, mariachi bands and especially, now, Angel Juan.

Angels in Mexico might all have black hair, Witch Baby thought. I might belong there.

"What's it like?" she asked, thinking of rose-covered saints and fountains.

"Where I'm from it's poor. Little kids sit on the street asking for change. Some of them sing songs and play guitars they've made themselves, or they sell rainbow wish bracelets. There are old ladies too—just sitting in the dirt. People come from your country with lots of money and fancy clothes. They go down to the bars, shoot tequila and go back up to buy things. It's crazy to see them leaving with their paper flowers and candles and blankets and stuff, like we have something they need, when most of us don't even have a place to sleep or food to eat. Maybe they just want to come see how we live to feel better about their lives, or maybe they're missing something else that we have. But you're different." He stared at Witch Baby. "Where did you come from?"

Witch Baby shrugged.

"Niña Bruja! Witch Baby! Cherokee and Raphael told me about you. What a crazy name! Why do they call you that? I don't think you're witchy at all."

"I don't know why."

"Who are your parents?"

Witch Baby shrugged again. She thought Angel Juan's eyes were like night houses because of the windows shining in them.

He sat watching her for a long time. Then he looked up at her wall with the newspaper clippings and said, "You need to find out. That would help. I bet you wouldn't need all these stories on your wall if you knew who you were."

Witch Baby took out her camera and looked at Angel Juan through the lens. "Can I?" she asked.

"Sure. Then I've got to go." Angel Juan winked at the camera and slid out the window. "*Adios*, Baby."

But Angel Juan came back. He and Witch Baby sat in the branches of the tree, whistling and chirping like birds. They went into the shed and he played My Secret Agent Lover Man's bass while Witch Baby jammed on the drums she hadn't touched for so long. Fireworks went off inside of her. Their lights came out through her eyes and shone on Angel Juan.

How could I not play? she wondered.

"They should call you Bongo Baby," Angel Juan said. "What does it feel like?"

"All the feelings that fly around in me like bats come together, hang upside down by their toes, fold up their wings, and stop flapping and there's just the music. No bat feelings. But sometimes the bats flap around so much that I can't play at all."

"Don't let them," said Angel Juan. "Never stop playing."

They made up songs like "Tijuana Surf," "Witch Baby Wiggle," and "Rocket Angel," and sometimes they put on music and danced—holding hands, jumping up and down, hiphopping, shimmying, spinning and swimming the air. They went to the tiny apartment where Angel Juan lived with his parents, Gabriela and Marquez Perez, and his brothers and sisters—Angel Miguel, Angel Pedro, Angelina and Serafina—and played basketball until it got dark, then went inside for fresh tortillas and salsa. The apartment was full of the lace doilies Gabriela crocheted. They looked like pressed roses covered with frost, like shadows or webs or clouds. Hanging on the walls and stacked on the floor were the picture frames that Marquez made. Some were simple wood, others were painted with blue roses and gold leaves; there were elaborately carved ones with angels at the four corners. Angel Juan and his brothers and sisters had drawn pictures to put in some of the frames, but most were empty. Everyone in the Perez family liked to hold the frames up around their faces and pretend to be different paintings. The first time Witch Baby came over and held up a frame, Angel Juan's brothers and sisters laughed in their high bird voices. They squealed at her hair and her name and her toes, but they always laughed at everyone and everything, including themselves, so she laughed too.

"Take our picture, Niña Bruja!" they chirped from inside one of Marquez's frames when they saw her camera.

The pictures of Angel Juan were always just a dark blur.

"Why do you move so fast?" she asked him. "You are even faster than I am."

"I'm always running away. Come on!" He took Witch Baby's hand and they flew down the street.

They flew. It felt like that. It was like having an angel for your best friend. An angel with black, black electric hair. It didn't even matter to Witch Baby that she didn't know who she was. At night she put pictures of an Angel Juan blur on her wall before she fell asleep.

Weetzie smiled when she saw the pictures. "Witch Baby is in love," she told My Secret Agent Lover Man. "Maybe she'll stop being obsessed with all those accidents and disasters, all that misery. It's too much for anyone, especially a child."

"Witchy plus Angel Juan!" Cherokee sang from inside her tepee. "Witch hasn't put up one scary picture for two weeks."

Witch Baby ignored Cherokee. She was wearing a T-shirt Angel Juan had given to her. Gabriela Perez had embroidered it with rows of tiny animals and it smelled like Angel Juan—like fresh, warm cornmeal and butter. The smell wrapped around Witch Baby as she drifted to sleep.

❤

"My pain is ugly, Angel Juan. I feel like I have so much ugly pain," says Witch Baby in a dream.

"Everyone does," Angel Juan says. "My mother says that pain is hidden in everyone you see. She says try to imagine it like big bunches of flowers that everyone is carrying around with them. Think of your pain like a big bunch of red roses, a beautiful thorn necklace. Everyone has one."

❤

Witch Baby and Angel Juan made gardens

of worlds. They were Gypsies and Indians, flamenco dancers and fauns. They were magicians, tightrope walkers, clowns, lions and elephants—a whole circus. They spun My Secret Agent Lover Man's globe lamp and went wherever their fingers landed.

"We live in a globe house."

"Our house is a globe."

"I am a Sphinx."

"I am a bullfighter who sets the bulls free."

"I am an African drummer dancing with a drum that is bigger than I am."

"I am a Hawaiian surfer with wreaths of leaves on my head and ankles."

"I am a dancing goddess with lots of arms."

"I am a Buddha."

"I am a painter from Mexico with parrots on my shoulders and a necklace of roses."

❤

And then one day Angel Juan wasn't on the set of *Los Diablos*, where Witch Baby always met him.

Somehow she knew right away that something was wrong. She hurled herself past Dirk and Duck's trailer, among the children Ping was painting, under the radiant blue archways that Valentine was building. The whole set and everyone on it seemed to pulse with blue, the blue of fear, the blue of sorrow.

"Angel Juan!" Witch Baby called. She jumped up and down at Valentine's feet. "Have you seen Angel Juan?"

Valentine shook his head.

"Angel Juan!" cried Witch Baby, tugging at Ping's sarong.

"I haven't seen him today, Baby Love," said Ping.

Dirk and Duck opened the door of their trailer. They didn't know where Angel Juan was either.

My Secret Agent Lover Man was directing the scene in which Coyote was dying of radiation in a candle-lit room. Witch Baby pulled on the leg of My Secret Agent Lover Man's baggy trousers with her teeth.

"Cut!" he said.

Coyote sat up and opened his eyes.

My Secret Agent Lover Man scowled. "I'm

busy now, Witch Baby. This is a very important scene. What do you want?"

"Angel Juan!"

"Angel Juan didn't come to the set today. I don't know where he is."

Witch Baby put on her skates and rolled away from the blue faces and archways as fast as she could. When she got to the Perez apartment, she felt as if a necklace of thorns had suddenly wrapped around her, pricking into her flesh.

Angel Juan was not there.

Angel Miguel, Angel Pedro, Angelina and Serafina were not playing basketball in the driveway. There weren't any baking smells coming from Gabriela's kitchen and there was no sound of Marquez's hammering. There was only a "For Rent" sign on the front lawn.

"Angel Juan!"

Witch Baby pressed her face against a window. The apartment was dark, with a few frames and doilies scattered on the floor, as if the Perez family had left in a hurry.

"I'm always running away," Angel Juan had

said. Witch Baby heard his voice in her head as she skated home, stumbling into fences and tearing her skin on thorns.

Weetzie was talking on the phone and biting her fingernails when Witch Baby got there.

"Witch Baby!" she called, hanging up. "Come here, honey-honey!" She followed Witch Baby into her room and sat beside her on the bed while Witch Baby pulled off her roller skates.

"Where is Angel Juan?" Witch Baby demanded. On her wall the pictures of Angel Juan were all running away—blurs of black hair and white teeth.

Weetzie held out her arms to Witch Baby.

"Where is Angel Juan?"

"I just got a call from My Secret Agent Lover Man. He found out that the immigration officers were looking for the Perez family because they weren't supposed to be here anymore. They went back to Mexico."

Witch Baby leaped off the bed and out the window.

She wanted to run and run forever, until she

reached the border. She imagined it as an endless row of dark angel children with wish bracelets in their hands and thorns around their necks, sitting in the dirt and singing behind barbed wire.

My Secret

Witch Baby was crying. Witch babies never cry, snapped a voice inside, but she couldn't stop. Angel Juan had been gone for two days.

Weetzie had never seen Witch Baby cry before and went to hug her, but Witch Baby curled up like a snail in the corner of the bed, burying her face in the embroidered animal T-shirt Angel Juan had given her. It hardly smelled like him anymore. Weetzie saw that the tears streaking Witch Baby's face were the same color as her eyes.

"Come on," Weetzie said, scooping her up.

Because Witch Baby was limp from the tears and the effort of trying to find Angel Juan in the T-shirt, her kicks and kitten bites did not prevent Weetzie from carrying her into the pink bedroom.

My Secret Agent Lover Man was in bed, reading the paper. He had never seen Witch Baby cry before either.

"What is it?" he asked gently, moving aside so Weetzie and Witch Baby could sit on the warm place. He reached out to stroke Witch Baby's tangles, but she shrank away from him, baring her teeth and clinging to the T-shirt.

"She wants to understand about Angel Juan," Weetzie said. "I thought you could explain."

My Secret Agent Lover Man scratched his chin.

"The Perez family came here to work, to make beautiful things. But our government says they don't belong here and sent them back again. It doesn't make a lot of sense. I'm sorry, Witch Baby. I wish there was something I could do. Maybe with my movies, at least."

"Angel Juan belongs anywhere he is," Witch Baby said. "Because he *knows* who he is."

"He is lucky then," said My Secret Agent Lover Man. "And he will be okay."

"Will I see him again?" Witch Baby whispered.

"I don't know, Baby. There are barbed wire fences and high walls to keep the Perez family and lots of other people from coming here."

Witch Baby crawled under the bed and began to cry loud sobs that shook the mattress. She felt like a drum being beaten from the inside.

My Secret Agent Lover Man got down on his hands and knees and tried to reach for her, but she was too far under the bed. She looked at him through a glaze of amethyst tears.

"Who am I?" she asked, clutching Angel Juan's T-shirt to her chest. "I need to know. You tell me."

My Secret Agent Lover Man turned to Weetzie, who was kneeling beside him and she reached out and took his hand. Then he looked at Witch Baby again. His face was dusky with worry.

"I didn't want to tell you because I was afraid you would be ashamed of me," he began. "I'm sorry, Witch Baby. I should have told you before. See, I've always thought the world was a painful place. There were times I could hardly stand it. So when Weetzie wanted a baby, I said I didn't want one. I didn't want to bring any baby angel down into this messed-up world. It seemed wrong. But Weetzie believed in good things—in love—and she went ahead and made Cherokee with Dirk and Duck. Or maybe Cherokee is mine. We'll never be sure who her dad really is. Well, you know all that.

"But then I got jealous and angry because of what Weetz had done, so I went away.

"While I was away I met a woman. She was a powerful woman named Vixanne Wigg and I fell under her spell. I didn't know what I was doing. Then something happened that woke me up and I left. I found Weetzie again, but I had been through a very dark time.

"One day Vixanne left a basket on our doorstep. There was a baby in it. She had purple tilty eyes.

"The only good thing about what happened with Vixanne Wigg was that we had made you, Witch Baby. I didn't want to tell you about it because I wasn't sure you would understand. But you're mine, Witch Baby. Not only because I love you but because you are a part of me. I'm your real father."

"And we all love you as if you were our real child," Weetzie added. "Dirk and Duck and I. You belong to all of us."

Witch Baby searched My Secret Agent Lover Man's face for her own, as she had always done. But now she knew. Tassellike eyelashes, delicate cheekbones, sharp chins. When he reached for her again, she let him bring her out from under the bed.

My Secret Agent Lover Man held Witch Baby against his heart, and she felt damp with tears and almost boneless like a newborn kitten. She closed her eyes.

❤

She is holding on to the back of his black trench coat that has the fragrance of Drum tobacco from Amsterdam deep in the folds. His back is tense and bony like hers but his shoulders are strong. She is strong too, even though she is small—strong from playing drums—he has told her that. He will take her with him down arrow highways past glistening number cities, telling her stories about when she was a baby.

"My baby, my child that lay on the doorstep smoldering. For such a young child—it frightened us to see that strength and fire. But I knew you. I remembered the way I'd seen the world when I was young. I'd seen the smoke and the pain in the streets, heard the roaring under the earth, felt the rage beneath the surface of everything, most people pretending it wasn't there. Only those who are so shaken or *so brave can wear it in their eyes. The way you wear it in your eyes."*

❤

They are both dressed in Chaplin bowler hats and turned-out shoes as they ride My Secret Agent Lover Man's motorcycle around a clock that is a moon.

Witch Hunt

The next morning Witch Baby woke at dawn and ran around the cottage naked, crowing like a rooster and dragging Rubber Chicken along behind her. Cherokee climbed out of her tepee and stood in the hallway rubbing her eyes.

"Witch, why are you crowing?"

"My Secret Agent Lover Man is my real dad," Witch Baby crowed.

"He is not," Cherokee said. "I know! He and Weetzie found you on our doorstep."

"He told me he's my real dad! He went away and met my mom and she had me and brought me here."

"He is *not* your dad!"

"Yes he is. He's my real dad but maybe not yours. You'll never be sure who your real dad is!"

Cherokee began to cry. "My Secret Agent Lover Man and Dirk and Duck are all my dads. None of them are yours!"

"My Secret Agent Lover Man is," said Witch Baby. "You have three dads but it's like not having any. You're a brat bath mat bat."

Cherokee ran to My Secret Agent Lover Man and Weetzie's bedroom. Her face and cropped hair were wet with tears.

"Witch says I'm a brat mat because I have three dads!"

My Secret Agent Lover Man took her in his arms. "Cherokee, you've known about that all your life. Why are you so upset now?"

"Because Witch says you're her real dad. I want one real dad if she has one."

"Honey-honey," Weetzie said, "My Secret Agent Lover Man is Witch Baby's real dad, but you get to live with your real dad and two other dads even if you aren't sure which is which. Witch Baby doesn't even get to meet her real mom. Think what that must be like."

Cherokee stopped crying and caught a tear in her mouth. She snuggled between My Secret Agent Lover Man and Weetzie, her hair mingling with Weetzie's in one shade of blonde.

None of them knew that Witch Baby was hiding at the doorway and that she had heard everything.

I'll meet my real mom! she told herself. I'll have two real parents and I'll know who I am more than Cherokee knows who she is.

The next morning Witch Baby put her baby blanket, her rubber-bug sneakers, her camera, Angel Juan's T-shirt and some Halloween candy she stole from Cherokee's hoard into her bat-shaped backpack, and she skated away on her cowboy-boot roller skates.

Later Weetzie and My Secret Agent Lover

Man woke up and lay on their backs, holding hands and listening for the morning wake-up crow. But this morning the house was quiet and Rubber Chicken lay limply by the bed.

"Where is Witch Baby?"

They looked at each other, looked at the globe lamp on the bed table, looked at each other again and jumped out of bed. They ran through the cottage, checking under sombreros and sofas, behind surfboards and inside cookie jars, but they couldn't find Witch Baby. They woke Dirk and Duck, who were surfing in their sleep in their blue bedroom, and told them that Witch Baby was missing. Cherokee came shuffling in, holding the puppy Tee Pee wrapped up like a papoose.

Duck pushed his fingers frantically through his flat-top. "I bet the witch child ran away!" he said.

Cherokee began to cry. "I've been so clutch to her."

"Let's go!" Dirk said, pulling on his leather jacket and Guatemalan shorts.

My Secret Agent Lover Man took the motorcycle, Duck took his blue Bug, Dirk took

Jerry, Weetzie called Valentine and Ping who got in Valentine's VW van. They drove in all directions looking for Witch Baby. They went to the candy stores, camera stores, music stores, toy stores and parks, asking about a tiny, tufty-headed girl. Cherokee and Raphael ran to Coyote's shack on the hill, chanting prayers to the sun and looking in the muddy, weedy places that Witch Baby loved. Brandy-Lynn stayed with Weetzie by the phone, while Weetzie called everyone she knew and peeled the Nefertiti decals off her fingernails.

Weetzie and Brandy-Lynn waited and waited by the phone for hours. Finally, Weetzie's fatigue swept her into a dream about a house made of candy. Inside was a woman with a face the color of moss who warmed her hands by a wood-burning stove. A suffocating smoke came out of the stove and there was a tiny pair of black high-top sneakers beside it.

Weetzie woke crying and Brandy-Lynn held her until the sobs quieted and she could speak.

"Witch Baby is in danger," Weetzie said.

"Come on, sweet pea," said Brandy-Lynn. "I'll make you some tea. Chamomile with milk and honey like when you were little."

They sat drinking chamomile tea with milk and honey by the light of the globe lamp and Weetzie stared at the milk carton with a missing child's face printed on the back. She read the child's height, weight and date of birth, thinking the numbers seemed too low. How could this missing milk-carton child be so new, so small? Weetzie imagined waking up day after day waiting for Witch Baby, not knowing, seeing children's faces smiling blindly at her from milk cartons while she tried to swallow a bite of cereal. Seeing a picture of Witch Baby on a milk carton.

"Where do you think she could be?" Weetzie asked her mother. "Would she just run away from us? Last time she was with Dirk and Duck."

Brandy-Lynn was staring at the clock on the wall and the pictures Witch Baby had taken. There they all were—the family—bigger and bigger groups of them circling the clock up to the number eleven. They were all laughing, hugging, kissing. In one picture, Weetzie and Brandy-Lynn were displaying their polished toenails; in one, Weetzie and Cherokee wore matching feathered headdresses; Ping was playing with Raphael's dreadlocks; Darlene was messing up Duck's flat-top. There were pictures of My Secret Agent Lover Man, Dirk, Valentine and Coyote. But there was no picture on the number twelve.

"Look at all those beautiful photographs," Brandy-Lynn said. "And Witch Baby isn't even on the clock. No matter how much we love her, she doesn't feel she belongs. You have me, Cherokee has you, but Witch Baby still doesn't know who her mother is."

"I've been a terrible almost-mother," said Weetzie. "I won't just stop and pay attention when someone is sad. I try to make pain go away by pretending it isn't there. I should have seen her pain. It was all over her walls. It was all in her eyes."

"It takes time," Brandy-Lynn said, fingering the heart locket with the shadowy picture of Charlie Bat. "I didn't want to let you be the witch child you were once. I couldn't face your father's death. And even now darkness scares me." She set down the bottle of pale amber liqueur she was holding poised above her teacup, and pushed it away from her. "I didn't understand those newspaper clippings on Witch Baby's wall."

"How will I ever be able to tell Witch Baby what she means to us?" Weetzie cried. "She isn't just my baby, she's my teacher. She's our rooster in the morning, she's . . . How will I ever tell her?" she sobbed, while Brandy-Lynn stroked her hair. But Weetzie could not say the other thought. Would she be able to tell Witch Baby anything at all?

Vixanne Wigg

When she left the cottage, Witch Baby skated past the Charlie Chaplin Theater and the boys in too-big moon-walk high-tops playing basketball at the high school. She passed rows of markets where old men and women were stooped over bins of kiwis and cherries. They lived in the rest homes around the block, where ambulances came almost every day without using their sirens. One old woman with a peach in her hand stared as Witch Baby took her photograph and rolled away.

At Farmer's Market she skated past stalls selling flowers, the biggest fruits she had ever seen, New Orleans gumbo, sushi, date shakes, Belgian waffles, burritos and pizzas—all the smells mingling together into one feast. At the novelty store she saw pirate swords, beanies and vinyl shoppers covered with daisies. There were mini license plates and door plaques with almost every name in the world printed on them. But there was nothing with "Witch Baby" or "Vixanne" on it. Witch Baby knew she wouldn't find her mother here, eating waffles and drinking espresso in the sunshine. So she caught a bus to the park above the sea.

Under palm trees that cast their feathery shadows on the path and the green lawns, Witch Baby photographed men in ragged clothes asleep in a gazebo, and a woman standing on the corner swearing at the sun. Near the woman was a shopping cart packed with clothes, blankets, used milk cartons, newspapers and ivy vines. Witch Baby took a picture and put some of her Halloween candy into the woman's cart. Two young men were walking under the palms. They looked almost like twins—the way they were dressed and wore their hair—but one was tanned and healthy and one was fragile, limping in the protection of the other man's shadow over a heart-shaped plot of grass. Because of the palm trees, for a moment, the healthy man's shadow looked as if it had wings. Witch Baby took a picture and skated to the pier lined with booths full of stuffed animals.

She rode a black horse on the carousel, made faces at the mechanical fortune teller with the rolling eyeballs and bought a hot dog at the Cocky Moon. Nibbling her Cocky Moon dog, she stood at the edge of the pier and looked down at the blue-and-yellow circus tent in the parking lot by the ocean. Weetzie and My Secret Agent Lover Man had taken Witch Baby and Cherokee to the tent to see the clowns coming out of a silvery-sweet, jazzy mist. The silliest, tiniest girl clown hid behind a parasol and was transformed into a golden tightrope walker.

Witch Baby thought of the old ladies and the basketball boys, the street people and the clowns, the tightrope walker goddess and the man who could hardly walk. She remembered the globe lamp burning with life in the magic shop. She remembered Angel Juan's electric black-cat hair.

This is the time we're upon.

She skidded down to the sand, took off everything except for the strategic-triple-daisy bikini Weetzie had made for her and jumped into the sea. Oily seaweed wrapped around her ankles and a harsh smell rose up from the waves, only partly disguised by the salt. Witch Baby thought of how Weetzie, My Secret Agent Lover Man, Dirk, Duck and Coyote had once walked all the way from town to bless the polluted bay with poems and tears. She got out of the water and built a sand castle with upsidedown Coke cup turrets and a garden full of seaweed, cigarette butts and foil gum wrappers. Then she took pictures of surfer boys with peeling noses, blonde surfer girls that looked like tall Cherokees, big families with their music and melons, and men who lay in pairs by the blinding water.

When evening came Witch Baby had a sun-burned nose and shoulders and she was starving. After she had eaten the sandy candy corn and Three Musketeers bars from her bat-shaped backpack, she was still hungry and it was getting cold.

I won't find my mother here, she thought, getting back on a bus headed for Hollywood.

She found a bus stop bench in front of the Chinese Theater and curled up under the frayed blanket in her backpack, the same blanket that had once covered her in the basket when Weetzie, My Secret Agent Lover Man, Dirk and Duck had found her on their doorstep. Shivering with cold, she finally slept.

The next morning Witch Baby waited until the tourists started arriving for the first matinee. She rolled backward, leaping and turning on her cowboy-boot skates over the movie-star prints in the cement all day, and some people put money in her backpack. Then she went to see "Hollywood in Miniature," where tiny cityscapes lit up in a dark room. Hollywood Boulevard was very different from the clean, ice-cream-colored miniature that didn't have any people on its tiny streets.

If there were people in "Hollywood in Miniature," they'd be dressed in white and glitter and roller skates, with enough food to eat and warm places to go at night, Witch Baby thought, watching some street kids with shaved heads huddling around a ghetto blaster as if it were a fire.

That was when she saw a piece of faded pink paper stapled to a telephone pole. The blonde actress in the picture pressed her breasts together with her arms and opened her mouth wide, but even with the cleavage and lips she looked small and lost.

"Jayne Mansfield Fan Club Meeting," said the sign. "Free Food and Entertainment! Candy! Children Welcome!" and there was an address and that day's date.

So Witch Baby ripped the pink sign from the telephone pole and took a bus up into the hills under the Hollywood sign.

♥

Witch Baby skates until she comes to a pink Spanish-style house half hidden behind over-grown-pineapple-shaped palm trees and hibiscus flowers. Some beat-up 1950's convertibles are parked in front. Witch Baby takes off her skates, goes up to the house and knocks.

The door creaks open. Inside is darkness, the smell of burning wood and burning sugar. Witch Baby creeps down a hallway, jumping every time she glimpses imps with tufts of hair hiding in the shadows, and breathing again when she realizes that mirrors cover the walls. At the end of the hallway, she comes to a room where blondes in evening gowns sit around a fire pit roasting marshmallows and watching a large screen. Their faces are marshmallow white in the firelight and their eyes look dead, as if they have watched too much television.

One of the women stands and turns to the doorway where Witch Baby hides. She is a tall woman with a tower of white-blonde hair and a chiffon scarf wound around her long neck.

"We have a visitor, Jaynes," the woman says.

Witch Baby feels herself being drawn into the firelit room. She stares into the woman's tilted purple eyes, a purple that is only found in jacaranda tree blossoms and certain silks, knowing that she has come to the right place.

"Are you Vixanne?"

"Who are you?" The woman's voice is carved—cold and hard. The necklace at her throat looks as if it is made of rock candy.

"Witch Baby Wigg, your daughter."

All the people in the room begin to laugh. Their voices flicker, as separate from their bodies as the shadows thrown on the walls by the flames.

"So this is Max's little girl. I wonder if she's as quick to come and go as her father was. Did Max and that woman tell you all about how he left me, Witch Baby?" Vixanne asks. Then she turns to the people. "Do you think my daughter resembles me, Jaynes?" She reaches up and removes her blonde wig, letting her black hair cascade down, framing her fine-boned porcelain face.

"Let's see how my baby witch looks as a Jayne blonde," she says, putting the wig on Witch Baby. "You need a wig with that hair, Witch Baby!"

The people laugh again.

"Now you can be a part of the Jayne Club." Vixanne leads Witch Baby over to the screen. Jayne Mansfield flickers there, giggles, her chest heaving.

"Sit here and have some candy," says someone in a deep voice, delicately patting the seat of a chair with two manicured fingers. Witch Baby can't tell if the thick, pale person in the wig and evening gown is a man or a woman.

Witch Baby sits up all night, gnawing on rock candy and divinity fudge, drinking Cokes, which aren't allowed at the cottage, and watching Jayne Mansfield films. After a while she feels sick and bloated from all the sugar. Lipstick-smeared mouths loom around her. Her eyes begin to close.

"I'll put you to bed now, Witch Baby Wigg,"

Vixanne says, lifting Witch Baby up in her powdery arms.

There is something about being held by this woman. Witch Baby feels she has fallen into an ocean. But it is not an ocean of salt and shadows and dark-jade dreams. Witch Baby's senses are muffled by pale shell-colored, spun-sugar waves that press her eyelids shut, pour into her nostrils and ears, swell like syrup in her mouth. A sea of forgetting.

Vixanne carries Witch Baby up a winding staircase to a bedroom and tucks her beneath a pink satin comforter on a heart-shaped bed. Then she sits beside her and they look at each other. They do not need to speak. Without words, Witch Baby tells her mother what she has seen or imagined—families dying of radiation, old people in rest homes listening for sirens, ragged men and women wandering barefoot through the city, becoming ghosts because no one wanted to see them, children holding out wish bracelets as they sit in the gutter, the dark-haired boy who disappeared. What do I do with it all? Witch Baby asks with her eyes. Vixanne answers without speaking.

We are the same. Some people see more than others. It gets worse. I wanted to blind myself. You must just not look at it. You must forget. Forget everything.

And Witch Baby falls into a suffocating sleep.

In the morning, Witch Baby is too weak to get up. Vixanne comes in dressed in perfumed satin and carries Witch Baby's limp body downstairs. The others, the "Jaynes," are already gathered around the screen, eating candy and watching Jayne Mansfield waving from a convertible. Witch Baby sits propped up among them, wearing a long blonde wig. Her eyes are glazed like sugar cookies; her throat, no matter how many sodas she is given, is parched.

Late that night she wakes in her bed. "How will I ever be able to tell her what she means to us?" says a voice. Weetzie's voice. "Weetzie," she whispers.

She stumbles out of the room to the top of the stairs and looks down. Vixanne and the Jaynes are still watching the screen and charring marshmallows over the fire pit. A soft chant rises up. "We will ward off pain. There will be no pain. Forget that there is evil in the world. Forget. Forget everything." Vixanne is holding herself, rocking back and forth, smiling. Her eyes are closed.

Witch Baby goes back into her room and packs her bat-shaped backpack. For a moment she stops to look at the pictures she has taken on her journey. The floating basketball boys. The old woman with the peach. The hungry men in the gazebo. The dying young man and his angel twin. A picture of a child with tangled tufts of hair and mournful, tilted eyes. She leaves the pictures on the heart-shaped bed, hoping that Vixanne will look at them and see.

Then she slips downstairs, past the Jaynes and out the front door. She sits on the front step, tying her roller skates, clearing her lungs of smoke, gathering strength from the night.

The mint and honeysuckle air is chilly on her damp face, awake on the nape of her neck as Witch Baby Wigg skates home.

Black Lamb
Baby Witch

When Witch Baby tiptoed into the cottage, she saw Weetzie and My Secret Agent Lover Man holding each other and weeping in the milky dawn light. They looked as pale as the sky. She stood beside them, close enough so that she could feel their sobs shaking in her own body.

Weetzie lifted her head from My Secret Agent Lover Man's shoulder and turned around. Blind with tears, she held out her arms to the shadow child standing there. Only when Witch Baby was pressed against her, My Secret's arms circling them both, did Weetzie believe that the child was not a dream, a vision who had stepped from the milk-carton picture.

Beneath the pink feather sweater Weetzie was wearing, Witch Baby felt Weetzie's heart fluttering like a bird.

"Will you tell everyone she's home? I need to be alone with her," Weetzie said to My Secret Agent Lover Man. She turned to Witch Baby. "Is that okay with you, honey-honey?"

Witch Baby nodded, and Weetzie put on her pink Harlequin sunglasses and carried Witch Baby out into the garden. The lawn was completely purple with jacaranda blossoms.

"Are you all right? We were so worried. Where did you go? Are you okay?" Witch Baby nodded, not wanting to move her ear away from the bird beating beneath Weetzie's pink feathers.

They were silent for a while, listening to the singing trees and the early traffic. Weetzie stroked Witch Baby's head.

"When I was little, my dad Charlie told me I was like a black lamb," Weetzie said. "My hair is really dark, you know, under all this bleach, not like Brandy-Lynn's and Cherokee's. I used to feel like I had sort of disappointed my mom. Not just because of my hair, but everything. But my dad said he was the black sheep of the family, too. The wild one who doesn't fit in."

"Like me."

"Yes," said Weetzie. "You remind me of a lamb. But you know what else Charlie Bat said? He said that black sheeps express everyone else's anger and pain. It's not that they have all the anger and pain—they're just the only ones who let it out. Then the other people don't have to. But you face things, Witch Baby. And you help us face things. We can learn from you. I can't stand when someone I love is sad, so I try to take it away without just letting it be. I get so caught up in being good and sweet and taking care of everyone that sometimes I don't admit when people are really in pain." Weetzie took off her pink sunglasses. "But I think you can help me learn to not be afraid, my black lamb baby witch."

When they went back into the cottage everyone was waiting to celebrate Witch Baby's return. My Secret Agent Lover Man, dressed like Charlie Chaplin, was riding his unicycle around the house. Dirk was preparing his famous homemade Weetzie pizza with sun-dried tomatoes, fresh basil, red onions, artichoke hearts and a spinach crust. Darlene Drake, who had arrived the day before, was helping Duck twist balloons into slinkster dogs. Valentine and Ping Chong presented Witch Baby with film for her camera. Brandy-Lynn lifted her up onto Coyote's shoulders.

"I think I saw five little Joshua tree sprouts coming up across the street," Coyote said, parading with Cherokee, Raphael, Slinkster Dog, Go-Go Girl and the puppies following him.

Then Coyote put Witch Baby down and knelt in front of her, like a sunrise, warming her face. "I'm sorry about the seeds. Even if they never came up, I shouldn't have been angry with you. We are very much the same, Witch Baby."

Everyone else gathered around.

"We want to thank you," My Secret Agent Lover Man said. "I've been remembering that night when the article and the globe lamp appeared, and I realized that they must have been from you." He scratched his chin. "I don't know how I didn't see that before. They are beautiful gifts, the best gifts anyone has ever given me. Gifts from my daughter."

"And I want to thank you, too," Darlene Drake said shyly, placing a slinkster dog balloon at Witch Baby's feet. "You knew more about love than I knew. You helped me get my son back again."

"Without you, Miss Pancake Dancer Stowawitch, we might never have really known each other," said Duck, stooping to kiss Witch Baby's hand.

"Welcome home, Witch," Cherokee said. "I don't even mind my haircut anymore. I deserve it, I guess, since I did the same thing to you once. And besides, I look more like Weetzie now!"

Witch Baby snarled just a little.

"And thank you for helping me and Raphael find each other," Cherokee went on. "While you were away, Raphael told me it was your drumming I heard that day. You are the most slinkster-cool jamming drummer girl ever, and we hope you will play for us again even though we are clutch pigs sometimes."

"Yes, play!" everyone said.

My Secret Agent Lover Man set up the drums.

"I had them fixed for you," he said. "My daughter, a drummer. I knew it!"

So Witch Baby played. Tossing her head, sucking in her cheeks and popping up with the impact of each beat. Thrusting her whole body into the music and thrusting the music into the air around her. She imagined that her drums were planets and the music was all the voices of growth and light and life joined together and traveling into the universe. She imagined that she was playing for Angel Juan, turning the pain of being without him into music he could hear, distilling the flowers of pain into a perfume that he could keep with him forever.

Everyone sat in the candlelight, watching and listening and imagining they smelled salty roses in the air. Some of their mouths fell open, some of their eyes filled with tears, some of them bounced to the beat until they couldn't stand it anymore and had to get up and dance. Weetzie put her palms over her heart.

When Witch Baby was finished, everyone applauded. Weetzie kissed her face.

"And now it is time for a picture," Weetzie announced.

Witch Baby started to get her camera, but someone had set it up already.

"Come here, Baby," My Secret Agent Lover Man said. "You are as good a photographer as a drummer, but you aren't taking this one. This picture is of all of us."

He put her on his lap and they all gathered around. Weetzie set the timer on the camera and then hurried back to the group.

The picture was of all of them, as My Secret Agent Lover Man had said—himself and Weetzie, Dirk and Duck and Darlene, Valentine and Ping, Brandy-Lynn and Coyote, Cherokee and Raphael and Witch Baby.

"Twelve of us," said Weetzie. "So the twelve on the clock won't be empty anymore."

"Once upon time," Witch Baby said.

At dinner that night, Witch Baby looked up at the globe lamp in the center of the table. Suddenly, as if a genie had touched it, the lamp bloomed with jungles and forests, fields and gardens, became shining and restless with oceans and rivers, burned with fires, volcanoes and radiation, sparkled with deserts, beaches and cities, danced with bodies at work in factories and on farms, bodies in worship, playing music, loving, dying in the streets, flesh of many colors on infinite varieties of the same form of bones. And there—so tiny— Witch Baby saw their city.

This is the time we're upon.

Witch Baby looked around the table. She could see everyone's sadness. Her father was thinking about the movie he was making—the village where everyone is poisoned by something they love and worship. Witch Baby knew he was haunted with thoughts about the future of the planet. Dirk and Duck prayed that a cure would be found for the disease whose name they could not speak. Brandy-Lynn had never gotten over the death of Weetzie's father, Charlie Bat, and Darlene was with Chuck because she could not face another loss like the loss of Eddie Drake. Coyote mourned for the sky and sea, animals and vegetables, that were full of toxins. Some people hated to see Ping and Valentine together, because they weren't the same color, and Cherokee and Raphael might have to face the same hatred. Cherokee would never know for sure who her real dad was. There was Weetzie with her bitten fingernails, taking care of all these people, showing them the world she saw through pink lenses. Somewhere in Mexico, separated from Witch Baby by walls and barbed wire, floodlights and blocked-off trenches, was the Perez family—Marquez, Gabriela, Angel Miguel, Angel Pedro, Angelina and Serafina, and Angel Juan—Angel Juan who would always be with Witch Baby, a velvet wing shadow guarding her dreams. And there was Vixanne trying to deny the grief she saw, trying to keep it from entering her body through eyes that were just like Witch Baby's eyes.

Witch Baby saw that her own sadness was only a small piece of the puzzle of pain that made up the globe. But she was a part of the globe—she had her place. And there was a lot of happiness as well, a lot of love—so much that maybe, from somewhere, far away in the universe, the cottage shone like someone's globe lamp, Witch Baby Secret Agent Black Lamb Wigg Bat thought.